The Princess and the Pea

Retold by Xanthe Gresham

Illustrated by Miss Clara

Barefoot Books
step inside a story

There was once a prince whose heart was skinless. It quivered like a leaf in the breeze and shone like sunshine on a drop of water. And sometimes such a faraway light would well in his eyes that the servants laughed behind their dusters.

One morning, the prince announced, "I am going to search the world for a true princess!" And with that, he clicked for the cat and called for his carriage.

He began to pile rare gifts on top. There were petticoats and parasols, packs of cards and gold rings, arrows, bows and china lamps, wooden globes and books of stamps. All for the true bride he was quite sure he would meet and for the people who would help him on his journey.

"Oh dear!" sighed the queen, looking at the rare and beautiful treasures. "He's so strong and yet so sensitive!"

"Just like you!" replied the king. "A cruel word can redden your cheek like a slap."

"Meow!" said the cat and gave them a glare. Then she trotted after the prince, her tail as straight as a sword.

With a rumble of wheels and a cloud of dust, the carriage set off. Every tree, every shower, every rock, every flower was such a wonder that they scratched his sensitive heart like a rough wool scarf. How he longed for a princess whose love would be like silk around it! But then his carriage went so fast that the sky was a blur.

His journey was long and perilous and the adventures so many that the prince forgot his heart, fighting tigers in the jungles and snakes in the deserts.

$\mathcal{A}$rrow-fast, the prince made his way east and came to the Kingdom of Lapis Lazuli. There was a princess with veils as soft as the clouds and a face as bright as the moon. He gave her a singing bird, but she opened up the cage and flung it to the sky with a harsh laugh that lashed at his heart. The prince shivered.

The cat shook and stretched, then leapt back into the carriage.

The prince rode on to the Kingdom of
Rubies and met a princess dancing.
As she moved, little bells on her ankles
rang with such sweetness that he ran up
and offered her a rose, but a breeze blew
it from his hands as the princess spun.

She crushed that flower beneath her
feet and the prince's heart crumpled.

The cat arched her back and
padded towards the carriage.

Lonely rode the prince, over moss and stones, far from home, his heart swelling like a storm cloud, until he came to the Kingdom of Amethyst and met the Princess of Scent. He was so drunk on the perfume of blossom that he swayed and stared at her, his heart shining brighter and brighter, until the princess snapped her parasol shut with a frown.

The prince's heart sank, like the sun behind the mountains. He followed the cat to his carriage, her tail swishing and her ears flicking.

Downcast, the prince rode on, through wind and gale and slashing hail until he came to the Kingdom of Diamonds, where there were as many princesses as there are stars in the sky or flakes in a snowstorm. Their crystal eyes were as hard as needles and so he hid his heart and kept his distance. The cat stayed safely in the carriage.

The prince knew it was time to go back home and yet he couldn't. A true prince doesn't fail in a quest.

Furious at his sensitive heart, the prince stopped in the Kingdom of Mountains. He shut himself up in an inn. How could he go home without a princess? Why did his heart hurt so? Alone and angry in his room, he cut and thrust and parried and slashed with his cane, dueling with sunbeams and fighting with shadows.

One day a princess of horses arrived in the courtyard of the inn and tethered her stamping pony. She walked tall and strong, with a stride in her step, and her hair smelled of fresh air.

The prince left his room and went downstairs to meet her. He bowed to hide his blushes. Then he cleared his throat, opened his mouth, shut his mouth and sat down. And although the cat jumped on his lap and pressed her claws in his thighs, he couldn't say a single word.

Finally, the horsewoman asked, "Is no princess good enough for you?"

Sadly, the prince made the long journey home.
As soon as the battered carriage came into sight,
the queen hurried to meet it. "Why are you alone?" she
began. The prince silenced her by holding up his hand.

"In this wild and whirling world, there are many
princesses," he said. "Some are fierce, some free, some
cold and some bold, but I couldn't speak to any of them."
And with that, he turned from her and strode into the castle.

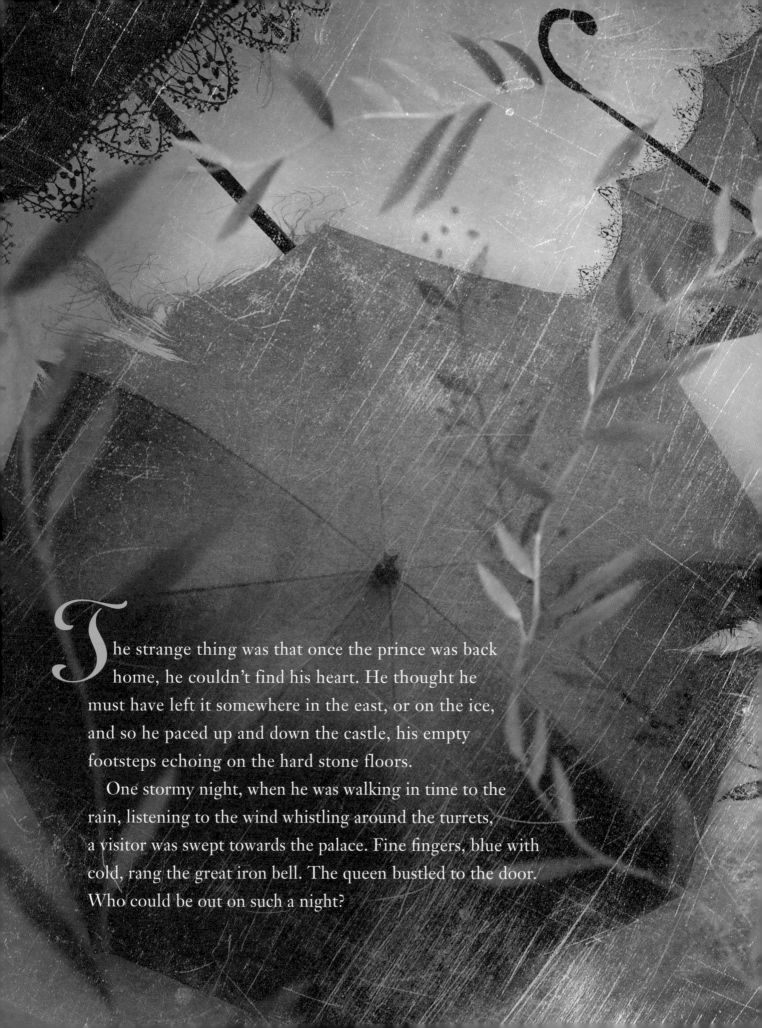

The strange thing was that once the prince was back home, he couldn't find his heart. He thought he must have left it somewhere in the east, or on the ice, and so he paced up and down the castle, his empty footsteps echoing on the hard stone floors.

One stormy night, when he was walking in time to the rain, listening to the wind whistling around the turrets, a visitor was swept towards the palace. Fine fingers, blue with cold, rang the great iron bell. The queen bustled to the door. Who could be out on such a night?

When the door opened, the prince caught sight of a girl. Her eyes were the same grey as the rain, her hair tangled with the petals of storm flowers and water flowed in and out of her shoes. He stepped back into the shadows and caught his breath, listening, as the stranger explained that her father and mother had died and she had nowhere to stay.

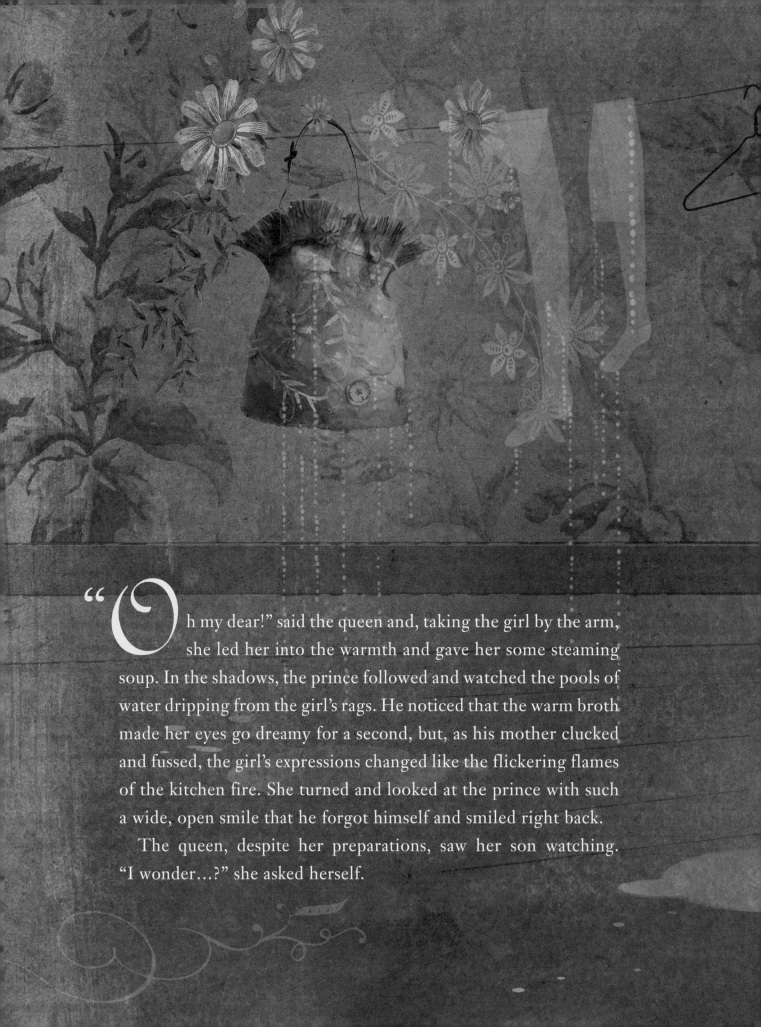

"Oh my dear!" said the queen and, taking the girl by the arm, she led her into the warmth and gave her some steaming soup. In the shadows, the prince followed and watched the pools of water dripping from the girl's rags. He noticed that the warm broth made her eyes go dreamy for a second, but, as his mother clucked and fussed, the girl's expressions changed like the flickering flames of the kitchen fire. She turned and looked at the prince with such a wide, open smile that he forgot himself and smiled right back.

The queen, despite her preparations, saw her son watching. "I wonder…?" she asked herself.

She was thinking and remembering. Remembering a test that she had undergone many years ago to prove that she was a true princess. She called the servants to prepare the room. She knew it well, but it hadn't been used for many years. In it was a fine four-poster bed, with twenty feather mattresses and twenty embroidered eiderdowns. The servants tutted at the dust and admired the silk, but when they had retired, out from a little golden box, the queen removed a single, ancient, hard little pea, and placed it under the mattresses.

PETITS POIS
extra dur

When the room was ready, the queen said, "Now my dear, you must take some rest," and led her to the room she had prepared. The girl stared for a second at the piles of mattresses, then clambered up the ladder, thanking the queen in a voice as happy as a lark, for the warmth, for the soup and for all her kindness.

But the next morning at breakfast, the girl was pale, her hair once more in tangles. "You look so tired!" said the queen. "How did you sleep?" At this the girl blushed and replied, "I'm really sorry, but I hardly slept a wink — the eiderdowns were lovely and your silks were rich and fine, but there must have been something hard in the mattress, because my skin is black and blue with tiny little bruises."

"That's terrible!" exclaimed the king. "And to think that a night with us has robbed you of your smile!"

Quietly, the girl replied, "It's not your fault. I'm sad because as I tossed and turned, I seemed to hear the voices of my mother and father, who I will never see again."

"And what did your parents say?" asked the prince, so softly that everyone turned, and the girl looked at him for a moment with her great grey eyes. "They said, 'Our daughter is a true princess.'"

"You are!" exclaimed the queen, clapping her hands. "Like my son and myself, for better or worse, you are sensitive in every way! I placed a pea beneath those piles of mattresses and it has found you out!"

The prince was on his feet, then on his knees. "I am yours if you will be mine! Every word from you, every glance, is like a silken scarf around my heart! Will you marry me?"

And after a beat that lasted as long as a blink, the girl replied, "I will!"

Then the cat began to caper and the king gave a secret smile and touched the queen's cheek, and as the girl had no family, they were married as soon as the preparations were complete.

And we were there too. We threw away our dusters and took our hearts to watch. And what a day it was! A day of each to his own, of crown and throne, of blossom on every cherry tree, of dancing to make us merry. And the true prince and his true bride, on rugs of petals side by side, threw golden coins as bright as the sun. When the wedding day was done, we took the coins home and bit them to test them, and the gold was so soft it didn't break our teeth.

*A*s for the pea, it was returned to the golden box and placed in the royal treasure cabinet. And it's still there — if no one has stolen it. As for me, I haven't had the time to try it yet.

For Robin and Georgie. "To find the fire
that warms you — seek it yourself."
— Xanthe Gresham

Barefoot Books   Barefoot Books
2067 Massachusetts Ave   29/30 Fitzroy Square
Cambridge, MA 02140   London, W1T 6LQ

Adapted from the fairy tale by Hans Christian Andersen
Text copyright © 2013 by Xanthe Gresham
Illustrations by Miss Clara, first published in France as
La Princesse au petit pois © Hachette-Livre / Gautier-Languereau, 2012
The moral rights of Xanthe Gresham and Miss Clara have been asserted

First published in the United States of America by Barefoot Books, Inc
and in Great Britain by Barefoot Books, Ltd in 2013
This paperback edition first published in 2017
All rights reserved

Graphic design by Louise Millar, London
Reproduction by B&P International, Hong Kong
Printed in China on 100% acid-free paper
This book was typeset in Linoscript and Janson
The illustrations were prepared as scale models,
which were photographed and digitally enhanced

ISBN: 978-1-78285-355-8

British Cataloguing-in-Publication Data:
a catalogue record for this book is available from the British Library

Library of Congress Cataloging-in-Publication Data
is available under LCCN 2013002481

1 3 5 7 9 8 6 4 2